Herbert

the Hedgehog

Written by
Lynn E. Mueller
and
Amity Pierce Buxton

Illustrated by
David Tinoco

CCB Publishing
British Columbia, Canada

From the Authors...

To anyone who has ever felt different and did not believe that any other person on earth could ever understand her or him...

To every friend who has ever helped and encouraged someone to share what was in his or her heart...

Most of all, to parents, family, and friends who have given and continue to give their unconditional love and support to those whose deepest thoughts are locked away deep inside...

This book was written just for you.

Herbert the Hedgehog
Copyright ©2014 by Lynn E. Mueller and Amity Pierce Buxton
ISBN-13   978-1-77143-143-9
Second Edition

Library and Archives Canada Cataloguing in Publication
Mueller, Lynn E., 1966-, author
Herbert the hedgehog / written by Lynn E. Mueller and
Amity Pierce Buxton; illustrated by David Tinoco. -- Second edition.
Issued in print and electronic formats.
ISBN 978-1-77143-143-9 (pbk.).--ISBN 978-1-77143-144-6 (pdf)
Additional cataloguing data available from Library and Archives Canada

All rights reserved. No part of this publication may be reproduced, stored in a retrieval system or transmitted in any form or by any means, electronic, mechanical, photocopying, recording or otherwise without the express written permission of the publisher. Printed in the United States of America, the United Kingdom and Australia.

Publisher: CCB Publishing
                British Columbia, Canada
                www.ccbpublishing.com

Herbert was no ordinary hedgehog, and we knew something was very different the day we brought him home. He just didn't fit. No matter how he tried, he couldn't get comfortable. Even his favorite game, Hide and Go Seek, was impossible to play. He was always spotted first.

He spent hours by himself in the thicket, picking blackberries and sometimes sketching his dreams of life on the open prairie, but, most of the time, just dreaming. One afternoon, aching inside, he packed his backpack and went for a very long walk to sketch, think, and sketch some more.

After making his way through lettuce, pea pods, peppers, and tomatoes, he hobbled along a cobblestone path, leaving awkward, muddy tracks. By the time he chose to rest, his shadow was so far ahead of him, he knew the sun would surely set before he could ever get back home. He hopped along the cobblestones until he couldn't hop anymore. The path ended.

When he looked up he saw the grandest Koi pond he'd ever seen. There were cloud-shaped pools with never ending winding walls that looked like stacked pancakes. Weeping willows towered along the banks, as the perfume of Japanese cherry blossoms filled the air. Speckled blue, orange, red, and white Koi flickered and glittered in the water against the setting sun.

"Hello," a voice echoed.

"Anybody there?" a Mallard Duck called out, paddling gracefully as he looked for a place to rest. "Yoo hoo!" he hollered, seeing the newcomer. "I'm Max."

"Hi!" Herbert shouted, dashing behind the rocks, too nervous to be seen, but relieved, just the same, to have company.

"I can't introduce myself properly if I can't see you," Max explained.

"I'm Herbert, and I'll stay here if it's just the same to you," he called out anxiously.

"Suit yourself." Max paused as a flood of questions poured into his mind, knowing Herbert wasn't a resident of the pond. "Aren't you far from home? Where do you live? How'd you find this place?" he inquired.

"I live back in the garden. Yes, I'm far from home. I'm not really sure how I found this place. I just took a walk and ended up here," Herbert admitted. Embarrassed, he wiped the tears from his eyes, feeling like he just needed to be alone.

"Do you have a family? Did you tell them where you were going?" Max asked, worried that Herbert would have a long walk home and nightfall was approaching quickly. He knew Herbert's family, too, would be worried.

"My family's back home in the burrow. It's surrounded by a lovely thicket in the garden. I didn't tell them I was leaving because I'm the only one who ever wants to leave. It's just me. I'm the only one who ever thinks of leaving," he whined.

"Why do you want to leave? What's troubling you?" Max asked, trying to be helpful.

"I just don't fit! I don't feel like I belong here -- I mean, at home in the garden." He paused only long enough to collect his thoughts and feelings and to search for a few stones to skip across the pond. "I have a wonderful family," Herbert cried, skipping a stone across the pond, "and a beautiful burrow." He skipped another as the Koi splashed and dashed, sending rippled waves onto the rocks. "I'm surrounded by the most delicious blackberries, but I don't feel like it's my home! I never have!" He yelled so loud, a cloud of birds filled the sky. "I just don't feel like I belong here. I love my mom and dad so much and I love my brother and sister. It's not them, it's me!" He cried, skipping the last stone so hard, it made it all the way across the pond. Herbert found a place to sit behind some rocks, buried his head in his paws and wept. "It's not them, it's me."

"Have you told them?" Max asked, paddling to the water's edge.

"Nope," he admitted.

"Don't you think you should?" Max nudged, knowing his own parents would never have let him go anywhere to a new place alone.

"Nope, well maybe, but I just can't. I don't want to disappoint them," he whimpered. "They love me so much. I couldn't bear to tell them I just want to leave."

"Well, when you do tell them and need a lift, let me know. I know where there are many lovely prairies."

"Well if I just fit in, it wouldn't matter!" Herbert sobbed.

Then there was a very long silence between them. It was such a long silence that Herbert was feeling uncomfortable. He stared at the ground and shuffled his feet.

Then, Max had something very important to say. "Well, to be honest, it makes perfect sense to me."

"What does?" Herbert looked up peeking through the rocks.

"How you're feeling makes sense."

"It does?" Herbert asked in awe. He stepped slowly out from behind the rocks.

"Sure, look at you." Max continued, "If I had to guess, you're bigger than your brother and sister aren't you?"

"Yes."

"You have a small tail?"

"Yes!" Herbert echoed, looking back at his tail, amazed that Max caught so much detail when he hadn't even formally introduced himself.

"I bet you have five toes on your back paws and just four toes on your front paws."

"I do!" Herbert yelled out, excited as he looked down at his feet.

"What's your favorite food?"

"Blackberries."

"Your family?"

"Mom and Dad aren't so keen on them. They say we live in a thicket because the thorns protect us. They say the berries are just there, but I love them! The rest of my family eats insects mostly, spiders and slugs. "Actually," Herbert paused, "I gotta say, slugs aren't bad. I've tried them."

"Well, this all makes perfect sense to me," Max said confidently.

"What does?"

"Why you feel different."

"It does?"

"Of course it does! You, my friend, were born this way and it's nothing to be sad about and, if I may say, without being rude, it's certainly nothing to leave home about."

"I don't understand." Herbert wept, finding a place to sit at the water's edge to talk to Max.

"You are unique to your family, and they're still your family, and they love you very much, don't they?" Max offered gently.

"They do."

"Well, I think you should talk to them. The ones you love will always be there for you, Herbert."

"I don't know if they'd understand."

"Have faith, Herbert! If you don't try to talk to them, you'll never know."

"Thank you!" Herbert said quietly. Max's words made a lot of sense. He had a lot to think about.

As the radiant orange sunset faded and dusk welcomed the evening sky, Herbert knew it was time to go. It was hard to leave this spot. Here, he felt safe.

"Will you be here tomorrow?" he asked Max.

"Of course!" Max smiled and added, "It's getting dark out. How will you be getting home?"

"The way I came, of course." Herbert replied.

"OK. I've talked to a few friends who live along your way home. They'll keep you company and light your path."

"Oh, thank you, Max! Thank you for your kindness."

"See you again soon, Herbert."

"Bye!" Herbert couldn't wait to get home, knowing he'd found a friend and a secret place to call his own.

As he walked, he thought to himself, "How do I tell them I just want to go to the prairie? They love me so much." Guided by the soft light of the fireflies, he searched the rocks for a place to rest before the long walk home.

Perplexed and without any more courage than he had before, he still knew Max was right and sat down beside the path among the fireflies, scribbling in his notebook the words he longed to tell his family. He felt worried knowing that leaving them would make them very, very sad.

As he wrote, he couldn't stop thinking about the beautiful waterfall back at the pond. There were so many rocks and crevices, it was the perfect place to think, sketch, daydream, and, most importantly, think of a way to tell his family what was in his heart.

"I think I'll keep my secret for now," he sighed, knowing that would be easier than sharing what was really in his heart. He put his notebook and pencil into his pack and headed home to us, his family.

And because Herbert couldn't bear to leave us, nor say a word to us, he suffered greatly back home. He was sad, knowing his dreams of living his life on the open prairie couldn't come true unless he shared what was in his heart.

And as time passed, he grew.

And grew...

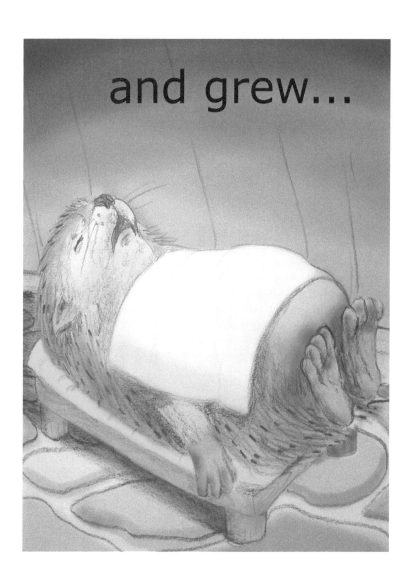

and grew...

And, the more he grew, the less he fit. The less he fit, the more he visited his hiding place at the Koi pond until one day, he didn't come home at all.

We were frantic when he didn't come home for supper. We rushed outside and searched for him everywhere.

And you know what? We saw him and froze.

He was looking through the window at the supper table. We couldn't tell if he was sad or angry. We just knew something was very wrong. He looked so hopeless and desperately lost, and we didn't want to scare him away. Finally, we gained enough courage, but just as we started to go to him, he heard our footsteps and scampered away.

"Herbert, come back!" Holly yelled.

"Herbert, please come home!" Henry yelled and ran after him.

But it was no use. Herbert was nowhere to be found.

We were so sad that he didn't feel he could talk to us or give us the chance to tell him that no matter what, everything would be okay. We were his family and we loved him.

So, we wrote a note for Herbert and put it in the window, hoping he'd read it and come inside. And you know what? He did!

The very next day, knowing he'd be going for his walk, we did our best to follow him.

He left us a pretty good trail, dropping a pencil and, luckily, old sketches which scattered about the cobblestone path. We thought it would be so hard to find him. It didn't take long at all.

He was hiding in a crevice among the rocks at the waterfall.

We begged him for his company. He wouldn't tell us what was wrong only that he needed to be alone to think.

"Herbert, we know!" Holly cried out in desperation, "We've seen your sketches!" She held up one of his drawings. It was an ocean of tall wavy brown grass blowing in the breeze, rolling hills and a deep blue western sky painted with long wispy and feathery clouds that the wind breathed across the plains.

Still, he wouldn't let us in.

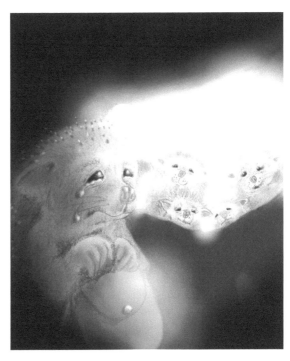

"I have an idea!" Holly took the pencil and a sheet of paper she'd found along the path, and began to write Herbert asking him to just come home, reassuring him that no matter what, everything would be ok.

We walked home without Herbert, just hoping he'd read our letter so that he'd know how much we loved him.

We felt betrayed, hurt, desperate, and terribly lost without our dear Herbert.

And then, the most peculiar thing happened! Can you guess what?

We met Max! We were so relieved to find out that Herbert had such a loving, caring, and wise friend. We told him how we've tried everything to talk to him and how, every time we did, he'd run away and hide. Max seemed to truly understand, and then he shared with us Herbert's troubles.

Once we realized why Herbert was so unhappy, we asked Max the most important question that anyone had probably ever asked him. "Would you be willing to take Herbert to the prairie?"

"I will when I know he's talked to you," Max replied, remembering Herbert's very important promise.

As seasons passed, no matter how hard we tried, nothing seemed to help.

Herbert just stayed in his deep, dark comfortable place for what seemed to be an eternity until....

Late one night, not long ago, we heard a strange rustling and bustling. We heard a sound we hadn't heard in what seemed to be years. It was the scurrying and hurrying of those wonderful clumsy steps that only our dear sweet Herbert could make.

Elated, we ran to him and found only this note. We couldn't believe he'd leave without seeing us first to say goodbye.

Dear Mom, Dad, Holly and Henry,

Thank you for loving me unconditionally when I could not love myself. Thank you for sharing your most important moments with me even when I was distant and in my comfortable place. I smiled often when I heard you laugh though I could not laugh myself. My heart aches for you, but I really need to go. I've been in this crevice for too many years. I've been in our garden much, much, too long. As long as I can remember I haven't fit in our home. Thank you for showering me with your kindness, compassion, and understanding. I'm sorry if I ever hurt you. I will always cherish you. Thank you for knowing my heart belongs on the open prairie and that I must find my way.

Love,
Herbert

Back in his crevice, Herbert packed his belongings ready to go.

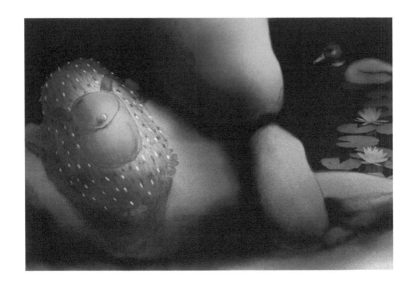

"There's no going back," he wept, angry for all his years of silence, angry that he allowed fear to run his life. Throwing his backpack over his shoulder, he scurried down the rocks, dreaming of his life on the open prairie.

Deep down, he desperately hoped his family would understand and that everything would be okay.

"Some day," he thought, "some day they'll know why I'm gone." He sat at the water's edge, glancing back for the very last time and then turned around, only to see Max swimming in the moonlight to greet him.

"Going somewhere?" Max called out from the shadows, having watched Herbert scurry down the rocks.

Herbert didn't reply.

"Need a lift?" Max extended his wing, keeping the promise he made so long ago. He knew Herbert's family would understand.

"No, thanks."

"You're sure?" Max nudged, knowing Herbert had his mind made up. He also wanted to make sure Herbert was safe.

"Well, okay," Herbert said quietly and climbed on.

Just as Max lifted his wings, all of us -- Dad, Mom, Holly, and Henry -- burst out of the shadows! "Herbert, wait!"

Herbert turned around just as Holly and Henry ran into his arms to hug him goodbye. "You mean you know?" he asked, looking into his mother's eyes with hope that she wasn't angry or disappointed.

"Yes, Son, we know."

Sobbing with relief, he buried his head in his mother's arms.

"Look, remember these?" Holly asked, holding up a drawing he did long ago.

"We saved them all!" Henry boasted, hugging his brother with sketches bundled under his arm.

"Every time we look at them, Son, we will think of you," said Dad. "We love you very much!"

We each gave Herbert one last goodbye hug. Max extended his wing, and Herbert climbed aboard.

"Thank you," he sobbed, as tears of joy flooded his eyes. For the first time in his life, he really understood that his family just wanted him to be happy. They had always been there for him and had been behind him all along. "I love you all so much!"

As Max paddled ready to take flight, Herbert sent kisses sailing through the air, making sure we caught each one.

"We love you, too!" we shouted, as Max stretched his wings to take flight.

"I'll be back soon! I promise!" Herbert called.

And his reassuring words were sealed in our hearts as our dear, sweet Herbert flew far, far away deep into the moonlit night.

After several hours of flying in the moonlight, Max asked Herbert, "Do you mind if we rest?"

"Not at all," Herbert replied.

"How about down there?" Max pointed to a clearing with a beautiful crystal lake. The moonlight danced on the water.

"Perfect."

Max glided on the lake, left Herbert on the bank, and then found himself a place to sleep.

Unable to rest, Herbert rummaged among the pictures and reminiscent odds and ends in his backpack and there was the family letter we had left for him so long ago.

Herbert closed his eyes. He didn't have to read it. Now aged and worn, he could hear our words in his heart.

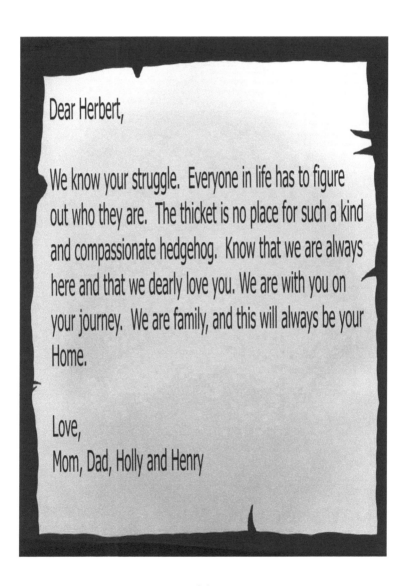

Dear Herbert,

We know your struggle. Everyone in life has to figure out who they are. The thicket is no place for such a kind and compassionate hedgehog. Know that we are always here and that we dearly love you. We are with you on your journey. We are family, and this will always be your Home.

Love,
Mom, Dad, Holly and Henry

The words echoed in his mind as he drifted off to sleep.

In a very short time, he awoke to find Max standing at the water's edge. Without a word, Max extended his wing. Herbert clambered on.

The moon and the stars shone brightly as Max took flight, as though they were filled with joy, knowing they were guiding Max to the place that Herbert really longed to be.

A message from Herbert

Have you ever thought you were different from everybody else? Have you ever been afraid to talk about it because you didn't think anyone would understand? I know exactly how you feel. I can tell you that the people in your life who love you most will always try to understand.

I learned that everyone feels different sometimes, and I've learned a lot more too! I've learned that not everyone will like the same things you do, and that's ok. I've learned that not everyone will want to do the same things you like to do, and it's ok. The most important thing I learned is that the ones who love you most will listen most, encourage you, and will always help you make good choices. Even when you can't find the words to say what's in your heart, the ones you love always seem to know just what to say and do to make you feel better. The ones you love are always there for you.

The best thing you can ever do for you is just always be yourself.

Love,

Herbert

Lightning Source UK Ltd.
Milton Keynes UK
UKHW050945220922
409236UK00001B/18